For my family and
for the people at Candlewick

Copyright © 1994 by Miko Imai
All rights reserved.
First edition 1994

Library of Congress Cataloging-in-Publication Data

Imai, Miko, 1963-
Lilly's secret / Miko Imai.—1st ed.
Summary: When Coco mentions Lilly's funny paws, Lilly is
afraid that her friend Joey will notice them too.
ISBN 1-56402-232-3 (reinforced trade ed.)
[1. Cats—Fiction. 2. Friendship—Fiction.] I. Title.
PZ7.I1156Li 1994
[E]—dc20   94-1

10 9 8 7 6 5 4 3 2 1

Printed in Hong Kong

The pictures in this book were done in watercolor and pencil.

Candlewick Press
2067 Massachusetts Avenue
Cambridge, Massachusetts 02140

Lilly's Secret

Miko Imai

CANDLEWICK PRESS
CAMBRIDGE, MASSACHUSETTS

Lilly was a little cat
who lived in a little house
in a little town.

One afternoon she was having tea
when her new neighbor Coco stopped by
and helped herself to a mouse biscuit.

"So, Lilly, did I see you with
Joey last night?"
"Yes," said Lilly. "We went
for a walk."

"Oh *really?*" said Coco.
"Has he noticed your funny paws?
They're so weird!"

Coco grabbed the
last biscuit and left.

Lilly felt terrible. No one had ever said anything about her paws before.

Suddenly they seemed really big and ugly.

She wanted to
cover them up.

But nothing
seemed to work.

That evening Joey came
over to her house.
"It's beautiful outside, Lilly.
Let's go for another walk."

"Oh no," thought Lilly.
"How will I hide my paws?"

"Hi, Joey," she said.

"Hello, Lilly. Don't you want
to hold my paw tonight?"

Lilly didn't know
what to say. She
shook her head
sadly. Then she
saw Coco.

"Hi, Lilly."

Lilly was sure
Coco had told the
other cats her
secret. What if she
told Joey too?

Lilly couldn't stand it anymore!

She ran and she ran

as fast as she could.

"What's the matter?"
Joey asked.

"Coco was going to tell
you about my paws. She
said they were weird. I
didn't want you to know
about them."

"Don't be silly, Lilly!
I've always known about
your funny paws.
I like them."

"Besides, you never said anything about my crooked tail!"